P9-AQA-921

for Annika, Elise, and Anja . . . always with you
— R.V.Z.

"Kim, come to me."
"Don't be afraid."
"I will always be with you."

Those are the only words I remember my mama saying to me. Three short sentences.

But I guess you remember words that are whispered at the bottom of a bombed-out crater.

Where once your house stood.
When you were four years old.
When you were alone.

Always with You

Written by Ruth Vander Zee

Illustrated by Ronald Himler

Eerdmans Books for Young Readers

Grand Rapids, Michigan / Cambridge, U.K.

Published in 2008 by Eerdmans Books for Young Readers,
an imprint of Wm. B. Eerdmans Publishing Co.
All rights reserved

Wm. B. Eerdmans Publishing Co.
2140 Oak Industrial Dr. NE, Grand Rapids, Michigan 49505
P.O. Box 163, Cambridge CB3 9PU U.K.

www.eerdmans.com/youngreaders

Manufactured in China

08 09 10 11 12   8 7 6 5 4 3 2 1

Library of Congress Cataloging-in-Publication Data

Vander Zee, Ruth.
Always with you / by Ruth Vander Zee; illustrated by Ron Himler.
p. cm.
Summary: Orphaned at the age of four when her village in Vietnam is bombed, Kim is rescued by soldiers and raised in an orphanage,
always finding comfort in her mother's last words — "Don't be afraid. I will always be with you."

ISBN-13: 978-0-8028-5295-3 (hardcover : alk. paper)
[1. Mothers and daughters — Fiction. 2. Orphans — Fiction. 3. Vietnam — History — 1945-1975 — Fiction.] I. Himler, Ronald, ill. II.
Title.
PZ7.V285116Alw 2008
[E] — dc22
2007009354

Display type set in ITC Tiepolo
Text type set in Della Robbia
Illustrations created with pencil and watercolor

In this story, "Vietnam" is spelled as one word, the preferred spelling today. However, Kim,
the narrator, would have spelled her country's name as two words, Viet Nam. Every word in
the Vietnamese language has only one syllable, no matter how many letters are in that word.

That day, Mama sent me to play under the umbrella of green coconut palms just outside my village.

A few moments later, the earth shook. The golden straw houses of my village exploded into orange clouds of fire.

When I finally dared crawl to where my mama might be,
I thought I heard my name.

I almost missed her words: "Kim, come to me."

I slid down into the deepness of a hole where my house
had been.

Mama held me close and whispered, "Don't be afraid."

Then she laid her hand on my head like a blessing,
breathing her last words, "I will always be with you."

I was alone.
All alone on that day.
That fiery day in my village in Vietnam.

Angry sounds tumbled, shout after shout, into
my not knowing what to do.
I heard, "There's one left alive," and then felt
the butt of a gun crack across the back of my head
on that day.
That blackout day in my village in Vietnam.

The soldier thought I was dead. But I wasn't.

I don't know how long I lay there, but when I woke, everything was hazy.

There were no colors. Nor have there ever been since that day.

I was thirsty. Real thirsty. My body hurt. My head throbbed on that day.

That gray day in my village in Vietnam.

In my mind, I heard my mama saying, "Don't be afraid, Kim. I will always be with you."

Then other sounds tumbled, word after word, into my not knowing what to do.

Kind words I did not understand from men I could not see.
I did not know them, but I did not fear them.
They carried me to their noisy machine and gave me sips of water. They said, "Here, Kim. Gum."

I chewed and chewed and chewed the gum's sweetness. It tasted like silvery sparklers in my mouth. Long after the sweetness was gone, I was still chewing. The gum would not go away. I thought to myself, "I will keep this gum forever."

I traveled with the soldiers for several days.
They made a soft bed for me. I felt stronger.
But when I rubbed my eyes, the world still didn't become
clear. At night, the darkness was darker than the gray of my day.

The soldiers said "orphanage" and "China Beach." I did
not know those words.

But one day they brought me to a place that would be
my home for the next five years.

They brought me to Ông and Bà Jones, whose love
helped me and hundreds of other children feel safe. Their
hearts must have been as big as barrels and filled with
every color of the rainbow.

I went to school. I perched on a bench at a table on the front porch of the orphanage. Cool breezes fanned our sun-bright faces. I could not see, but my best friend Vinh helped me learn.

After school, I would make my way to the sandy beach
where Vinh and I splashed in the water. We'd sing, "Bluebird,
bluebird in and out the window. Oh, Johnny, I am tired." We'd
shout, "Hey, bluebird, are you tired yet?"

Our answer was always, "Not yet!"
During the day, Vinh and I were two bluebirds playing our bluebird games.

At night, I cried for my mama.

Ông or Bà would come when they heard me crying. They would sit next to me on my bed.

"Kim, we can't bring your mama back to you. But you are safe here. Don't be afraid."

"Don't be afraid." My mama's words.

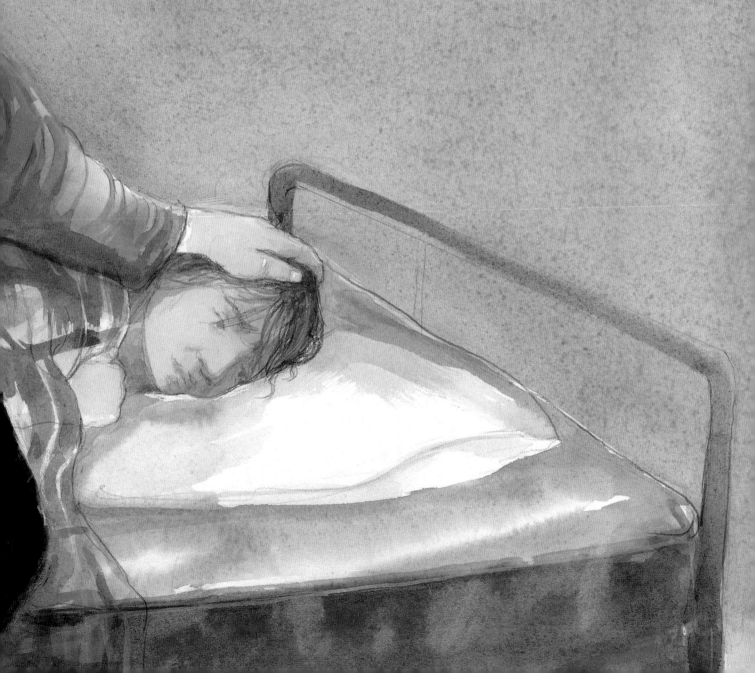

I spoke those words to my first baby doll, who arrived in a wooden crate from a faraway place.

I kissed her soft face, held her close to me, laid my hand on her head like a blessing, and said, "Don't be afraid. I will always be with you." I imagined her brown eyes, full of light, smiling at me.

I don't know how I felt safe when I was five, and six, and seven, and eight, and nine years old. But I did.

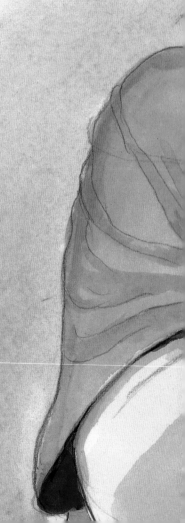

How do you feel full when there is not enough food to eat? When the rice and fish and hot pepper sauce are gone and you suck on buttons?

How do you feel sheltered when you are memorizing, "Even though I walk through the valley of the shadow of death, I will fear no evil," and bombs are exploding in the distance?

How do you feel secure when the dreams of your mama disappear in the dawn of the day? When you realize your only family is two loving people and hundreds of brother and sister orphans?

How do you see color in spite of the hazy gray?

I hear my mama's words, "I will always be with you."
I feel her hand on my head like a blessing.

And I am not afraid.